KT-195-783

Naggy
Aunt Aggie

First published in 2011
by Wayland

Text copyright © Liss Norton
Illustration copyright © Michael Garton

Wayland
338 Euston Road
London NW1 3BH

Wayland Australia
Level 17/207 Kent Street
Sydney, NSW 2000

The rights of Liss Norton to be identified as the Author
and Michael Garton to be identified as the Illustrator of this Work have
been asserted by them in accordance with the Copyright, Designs and
Patents Act, 1988.

All rights reserved

Series Editor: Louise John
Editor: Katie Powell
Cover design: Paul Cherrill
Design: D.R.ink
Consultant: Shirley Bickler

A CIP catalogue record for this book is available from the British Library.

ISBN 9780750263450

Printed in China

Wayland is a division of Hachette Children's Books,
an Hachette UK Company

www.hachette.co.uk

Naggy
Aunt Aggie

Written by Liss Norton
Illustrated by Michael Garton

WAYLAND

BUCKS COUNTY LIBRARIES	
066309536 %	
PET	
	27-May-2011
£4.99	GRM

One Saturday morning, Skelly Nelly and Bony Tony were eating their breakfast when the doorbell rang.

"I'll get it!" called Bony Tony,
racing to the castle door.

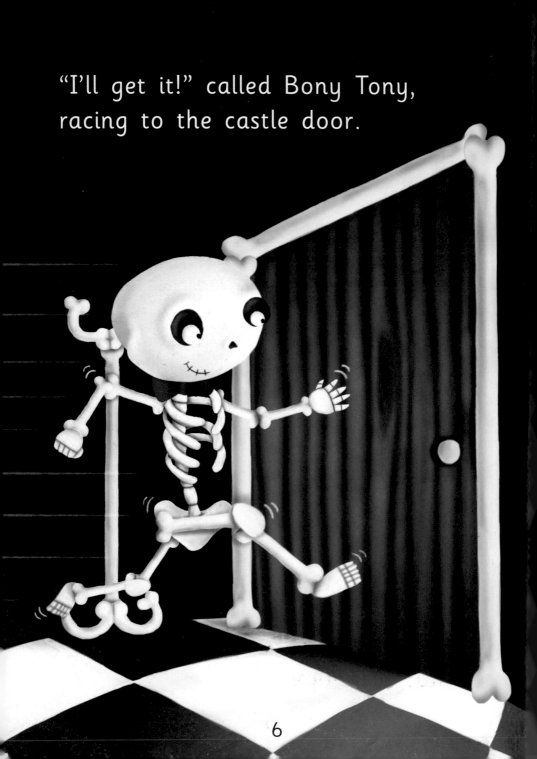

"A letter for you," said the
postman, giving Bony Tony
a small envelope.

"Oh, no!" groaned Bony Tony, as he read the letter.

"What is it?" asked Skelly Nelly.

"Naggy Aunt Aggie's coming to stay," he wailed, "for a whole week!"

Aunt Aggie arrived that afternoon.

"Well, I must say, this castle's a mess," she tutted, sweeping into the hallway. "Nelly, hang up those coats. Tony, put away those books."

Skelly Nelly and Bony Tony were
kept busy all day, cleaning and
dusting the castle.

Bony Tony was cleaning the kitchen when suddenly, he had an idea.

He picked up his bucket of dirty water and whispered to Skelly Nelly, "I'm going to balance this on top of the kitchen door so that it tips all over Aunt Aggie."

Just as Bony Tony stood on a stool to reach the door, Aunt Aggie burst into the kitchen. Bony Tony fell off the stool with a thud, tipping water all over himself!

"What a mess!" tutted Aunt Aggie.

Then, while Skelly Nelly was cooking dinner, she had another idea.

Skelly Nelly crept out of the kitchen and down into the cellar to catch some creepy crawlies.

She stirred them into Aunt
Aggie's stew.

"Creepy crawly stew will make her
go home," she whispered.

But Aunt Aggie didn't notice the creepy crawlies. She ate every bit of her dinner.

"Delicious! Now do the washing up," she shouted. "And after you've finished, you can both clean the bathroom. I want a bath."

Bony Tony and Skelly Nelly
stomped upstairs to clean
the bathroom.

As he scrubbed the bath, Bony Tony
saw a big black spider scurrying
towards the drain.

Bony Tony scooped the spider up
into his hands and showed it to
Skelly Nelly.

"Look what I've found," he whispered.

"Let's put it in Aunt Aggie's bed!" said Skelly Nelly. "That'll scare her away!"

Bony Tony and Skelly Nelly went into Aunt Aggie's bedroom. Bony Tony pulled back the bedclothes and put the spider in her bed.

"I hope this works," whispered Skelly Nelly.

Bony Tony and Skelly Nelly waited for Aunt Aggie to have her bath before going to bed.

When Aunt Aggie's bedroom door
clicked shut they held their breath.

It wasn't long before Bony Tony
and Skelly Nelly heard a scream.

"I think Aunt Aggie's found our
spider," laughed Bony Tony.

Sure enough, Aunt Aggie ran out of her bedroom.

"There's a spider in my bed!" she shrieked. "I hate spiders! I'm not staying here!"

Aunt Aggie ran downstairs and out of the front door.

"She won't come back in a hurry," cried Bony Tony.

"Hurray!" cheered Skelly Nelly.

START READING is a series of highly enjoyable books for beginner readers. **The books have been carefully graded to match the Book Bands widely used in schools.** This enables readers to be sure they choose books that match their own reading ability.

Look out for the Band colour on the book in our Start Reading logo.

The Bands are:

Pink Band 1A & 1B

Red Band 2

Yellow Band 3

Blue Band 4

Green Band 5

Orange Band 6

Turquoise Band 7

Purple Band 8

Gold Band 9

START READING books can be read independently or shared with an adult. They promote the enjoyment of reading through satisfying stories, plays and non-fiction narratives, which are supported by fun illustrations and photographs.

Liss Norton loves growing organic fruit and vegetables in her garden in the Sussex countryside, as well as spending time with her grandchildren, Maddie, Arabella, Dominic and Theo. When she's not writing, gardening or grandchildren-ing, she likes visiting castles. One day she hopes to find a secret passage...

Michael Garton lives with his girlfriend Leanna and a dalmatian puppy called Kiba. He works from his creepy flat on the Wirral in England (it's not quite a castle yet but he's saving up for one). He has been illustrating children's books since 2004 and thinks that everyone should have as many creepy experiences as possible.